Weekly Reader Books presents

NO MORE MONSTERS FOR ME!

by Peggy Parish

pictures by Marc Simont

An I CAN READ Book®

HARPER & ROW, PUBLISHERS

This book is a presentation of Weekly Reader Books.
Weekly Reader Books offers book clubs for children from
preschool through high school.

For further information write to:
Weekly Reader Books
4343 Equity Drive
Columbus, Ohio 43228

No More Monsters for Me!
Text copyright © 1981 by Margaret Parish
Illustrations copyright © 1981 by Marc Simont
All rights reserved. No part of this book may be
used or reproduced in any manner whatsoever without
written permission except in the case of brief quotations
embodied in critical articles and reviews. Printed in
the United States of America. For information address
Harper & Row, Publishers, Inc., 10 East 53rd Street,
New York, N.Y. 10022. Published simultaneously in
Canada by Fitzhenry & Whiteside Limited, Toronto.

Library of Congress Cataloging in Publication Data
Parish, Peggy.
  No more monsters for me!

  (An I can read book)
  Summary: Minneapolis Simpkin is not allowed to have
a pet, so she finds the most unusual replacement.
  [1. Monsters—Fiction.   2. Pets—Fiction]
I. Simont, Marc.   II. Title.   III. Series: I can read
book.
PZ7.P219No 1981   [E]   81-47111
ISBN 0-06-024657-X   AACR2
ISBN 0-06-024658-8 (lib. bdg.)

For Adele Hanna—with love.

"Not even a tadpole,

Minneapolis Simpkin,"

yelled Mom.

"And I mean it!"

"Okay, okay,"

I yelled back.

5

Mom and I always yell a lot.

But this time,

she was really mad.

And so was I.

I stamped out of the house.

I did not care

what Mom said.

I was going to have a pet.

I would take a long walk

and think about this.

So I walked

down the road.

Suddenly I heard

a funny noise.

The noise came

from the bushes.

I stopped and listened.

"Something is crying,

Minneapolis Simpkin,"

I said to myself.

"I will find out

8

what it is."

I looked in the bushes.

Was I surprised!

"Wow! A baby monster!"

I yelled.

I looked at the monster.

It looked at me.

Then it ran to me.

I put my arms around it.

"Don't cry," I said.

"Minneapolis Simpkin

will help you."

The monster stopped crying.

We stood there

hugging each other.

"A monster for a pet?"

I asked.

Mom never said no

to a monster.

But I never asked her that.

Will she say yes?

I needed time

to think about this.

But there was no time.

It started raining.

The monster did not like it.

It started bawling.

And I do mean bawling!

"Okay, okay," I said.

I grabbed the monster.

I ran home with it.

Mom was in the kitchen.

She did not see me.

But she heard me.

"Are you wet?" she asked.

"Yes," I said.

"Hurry and get dry,"

she said.

"Supper is about ready."

I ran to my room.

"So far, so good,"

I said to myself.

"But what now,

Minneapolis Simpkin?"

14

I shook my head.

I did not know.

"Minn," yelled Mom,

"supper is ready."

"Coming," I yelled back.

I started to go down.

The monster came, too.

"No," I said.

"You can't come."

I put the monster

in my closet.

It started bawling again.

What was I going to do?

I looked all around.

"My teddy bear!" I said.

I got the teddy bear.

"Here," I said.

The monster grabbed the bear.

It stopped crying.

I ran down to supper.

Mom had made a good supper.

Then I thought of something.

Monsters have to eat, too.

"Mom," I said,

"what do monsters eat?"

"Food, I guess," said Mom.

"But what kind?" I asked.

"Oh," said Mom.

"Is this a new game?"

19

Mom loves to play games.

So I said, "Yes."

"Let me think," said Mom.

"What *do* monsters eat?"

I was glad to let her think,

because I saw something.

I saw the monster.

"I will be right back,"

I yelled.

"I have to get something."

I had to get something, all right.

I had to get the monster hidden.

I grabbed the monster.

I took it to the basement.

The monster started crying again.

"Quiet!" I said.

"If Mom hears you,

we are in for it."

I grabbed an apple.

"Here," I said.

The monster took the apple.

It stopped crying.

22

I grabbed another apple.

I ran back to the table.

"Here, Mom," I said.

I gave the apple to her.

"What is this for?"

she asked.

I didn't know what to say.

But I had to say something.

"Because I love you," I said.

Mom laughed.

"Minneapolis Simpkin," she said,

"I love you, too."

Then Mom said, "Pickles!"

"Pickles?" I said.

"Of course," said Mom.

"Monsters love pickles."

"I didn't know that," I said.

Then I asked,

"Do you know where monsters live?"

"Yes," said Mom.

"They live in caves.

Deep dark caves."

"Gee, Mom," I said.

"You know a lot about monsters."

"I love monster stories,"

said Mom.

"I read lots of them."

Did Mom like real monsters, too?

I started to ask her.

But I didn't.

The basement door was opening.

"I will be right back, Mom,"

I yelled.

"Minneapolis Simpkin!"

yelled Mom.

"Can't you sit still?"

"Hic-cup, hic-cup!"

Oh, no!

The monster had hiccups.

"Now you have hiccups,"

yelled Mom.

"I will get some water,"

I yelled back.

"HIC-CUP! HIC-CUP!"

I opened the basement door.

My eyes almost popped out.

"You grew!" I yelled.

"What did you say?"

asked Mom.

"Nothing," I said.

I pushed the monster

back into the basement.

It was awful.

The monster was huge.

It was all lumpy.

"HIC-CUP! HIC-CUP!"

I got some water.

"Drink this," I said.

The monster drank the water.

The hiccups stopped.

"Minn," yelled Mom,

"please bring me

another apple."

"Okay," I yelled back.

But there were

no more apples.

Now I knew

why the monster was lumpy.

I grabbed a potato.

The monster

grabbed it from me.

I grabbed another one

and ran.

I locked the basement door.

"Here, Mom," I said.

"Minn, this is a potato,"

said Mom.

"I asked for an apple."

"Oh, sorry, Mom," I said.

"Minn," said Mom,

"why are you so jumpy?

Is something wrong?"

Something wrong?

Was it ever!

But maybe Mom could help.

So I said, "I am fine.

Tell me some more about monsters.

Where are those caves?"

"Up in the hills," said Mom.

"But don't bother

to look for one."

"Why not?" I asked.

"They are all hidden," she said.

"Only monsters can find them."

"Are you sure?" I asked.

"That is what

my mother told me,"

said Mom.

"I looked and I looked.

I never could find one."

I sure hoped Mom was right.

I had to get that monster home.

It was not a good pet.

Then it happened.

CRASH!

Mom jumped up.

"What was that?"

she asked.

Then she looked at me.

"Minn," she said,

"you were in the basement."

I nodded my head.

"Did you bring home

an animal?"

I nodded my head again.

"Minneapolis Simpkin!"

yelled Mom.

"I said NO PETS!"

"It is not a pet!"

I yelled back.

"Then what is it?"

yelled Mom.

I did not mean to.

I did not want to.

But I started bawling.

"It is a monster!"

I bawled.

I waited for

Mom to yell.

But she didn't.

"Oh, Minn," she said.

"You really need a pet,

don't you?"

"Yes," I bawled.

"But I want a kitten

or a puppy.

I don't want a monster."

"No," said Mom.

"A monster is not a good pet."

I stopped bawling.

"Now," said Mom

"go and close that window."

"Window! What window?"

I asked.

"The basement window,"

said Mom.

"I must have left it open."

I just looked at her.

I still did not understand.

"Minneapolis Simpkin!"

said Mom.

"The wind is blowing hard.

It blew something over.

That is what made the noise.

Go close the window."

I went.

There was a window open.

The potato basket

was turned over.

The potatoes were all gone.

47

But the monster

was still there.

It was sleeping.

I looked at it.

How would I ever

get it out of the basement?

It was getting

bigger and bigger.

I went back to Mom.

"I closed the window,"

I said.

"The monster is there.

But it is sleeping."

"Okay, Minn, you win,"

said Mom.

"I was wrong.

I will make a deal.

You get rid of your monster,

and you can have

a real pet.

Deal?"

"Deal!" I cried.

That monster was no pet.

But it was real.

"Good," said Mom.

"I am going to take

a long bath.

You get rid of

your monster."

"Sure, Mom," I said.

I was not sure.

But I was sure

going to try.

I woke up the monster.

"Come on," I said.

"We are going."

The monster came.

It had to crawl

through the doors.

And I had to push

from behind.

But we made it.

I headed for the hills.

The monster followed.

The night was very dark.

I don't like the dark.

But I had to get

that monster home.

We got to the hills.

The monster looked at them.

It made happy noises.

"Is this your home?"

I asked.

The monster turned to me.

Suddenly

we were hugging each other.

Then the monster

ran up the hill.

I felt good.

The monster

had found its home.

"No more monsters for me,"

I said.

I ran all the way home.

Mom was yelling for me.

I went into the house.

"Minneapolis Simpkin!"

yelled Mom.

"Where have you been?"

"Getting rid of the monster,"

I yelled back.

"That is what

you told me to do."

I started to bawl again.

Mom looked at me

in a funny way.

She hugged me.

Then I knew.

I knew Mom didn't believe

that monster was real.

But Mom kept our deal.

We went to the pet shop.

Mom really surprised me.

She bought two kittens.

"Two!" I said.

"Sure," said Mom.

"One for you,

and one for me."

"Mom," I said,

"you are okay."

"And so are you, Minn,"

said Mom.

We each took a kitten.

And we went home.